Copyright © 2019 by Mae Scott

Acknowledgments

I want to thank God first of all. Without Him, none of this would have happened. It would have remained a dream. I want to thank my mom and the rest of my family for all their love and support. A special thanks to my lil' sis, Gina, who was there from the beginning to the end. Thanks also to one of my favorite teachers Bonnie Wilson. My Childhood friend Tameka Miller. And last but not least, thank you the reader for taking the time to read and enjoy *When a Sista's Fed Up*.

Mae Scott

Chapter One

Waking up in Kenneth's arms made me feel grateful and loved, to have him in my life. I couldn't imagine or believe he would be leaving in a couple of more days to go to college up north. He suggested that I come along with him. As bad as I wanted to leave with him, I turned the offer down. Kenneth looked a little disappointed. How could I leave my family and friends behind? Besides, I had really big plans, which was to save up money for my own beauty salon.

Kenneth kissed me on the cheeks and slowly got out of bed. As he started putting his pants on, I could hear my mom calling my name. Kenneth wrapped his big, muscled arms around me, squeezing me the way that you would squeeze juice out of an orange. I looked into his big brown eyes while rubbing my fingers through his black wavy hair, saying, "I love you" in his ear.

After Kenneth sneaked out of my bedroom window, my mom opened the door. "Why are standing there and looking out the window? Didn't you hear me calling your name? Kids today." she would say. I didn't realize that I was still a child. Except for her child, maybe that's what she meant. My mom started picking my shoes off the floor and putting them in the closet, saying "Your friend, Nicole, called earlier." *What does she want*, I thought. Mom looked at me saying

"She said not to come pick her up for school today. She sounded sick." *Sick?* I thought. "I mean, what's wrong?" "I don't know," my mom said, closing the door.

Nicole and I had been friends since first grade and she had never missed a day of school. Besides, we only had a week of school left and tests to take. "Nicole," I said in an angry tone, "This is not a job, it's school. Something that will help you get a good job in the future, or perhaps further your career."

"I just don't want to see him today." Nicole said, crying.

"I understand that you're hurt so just turn your head, or walk the other way if he tries to pass you by." I was always there to comfort Nicole when she went through breakups that would eventually make up. But today just wasn't the day or the right time to be listening to Nicole whine over her ex. "I'll be there to pick you up in 40 minutes." I said, hanging up the phone.

After my bath, I walked downstairs to talk with my mom about getting my own place. She gave me the 'maybe' look, saying, "Afterwards, maybe." Usually, that means 'no' when it's coming from her. You would think she would try to help me out to get me out of her hair. But she said instead, "If you want your own place then you need to save up the money and get it yourself." She didn't understand I already was going to school full time and had a job on the side. I just needed a ladder to make it to the top and she couldn't even give me a lift. My mom raised me to be independent and not to rely on anyone but myself.

"You're the only one that can make your dreams come true by working hard for whatever you wish to accomplish. As smart, bright, and intelligent as you are, you can't possibly disappoint yourself, but others can disappoint you. My point is, that my mom raised me to be independent and that's how I'm going to raise you. And don't think for a second that I hate you. Trust me, I love you more than myself. It took late nights, heartaches, headaches, and a whole lot more for me to have the job and the things that I have today."

I couldn't argue with her about that. My mom was always busy writing articles, and my dad died when I was 12. I always wondered what he was like. *Probably selfish and stubborn, like me*, I thought.

I kissed my mother on the cheeks and walked out the door. While driving my white Oldsmobile car, Kenneth's and my song began playing on the radio, which led me into thinking about us. Even if things wasn't to work out between us, with him being so far away, I wanted to get down on my knees and beg him to stay. But I knew he was leaving for all the right reasons. One was to better his career, which I couldn't argue with him about that, or compete. I just didn't want to take the chances of him falling in love with someone else. If that was to happen, then I guess we were not meant to be. Besides, my mom always said life goes on with or without someone being in it. I didn't want to imagine Kenneth not being in my life. It just wouldn't be complete without him.

While pulling up in Nicole's driveway, I could see her peaking out the window. I started blowing my horn until I seen her walk out the door, with who knows what on.

"What is up with your clothes?"

"It's just something old."

"It looks like you just robbed the dead."

"You're the one making me go to school, so therefore I don't care what I have on." Nicole looked at me and said, "I feel so bad."

"Why do you feel so bad? He treated you like shit, Nicole. You deserve so much better. He's a fool for not wanting you in his life. But you're a bigger fool for letting him make you look and feel this way. What I'm trying to say is, while you're down, trust me, he's not. So please go inside and put something on that says 'I'm happy and no break up is going to get me down'."

Nicole sniffed her nose, saying, "I don't know what I would do without you!"

As we arrived at school, I could tell that Nicole was nowhere close to getting over Alex. She stayed in the car until she seen Alex and his friends disappear inside the building. "Come on, Nicole! We're going to be late for Mrs. Kimberley's class!"

There were lots of rumors going on around campus about Mrs. Kimberley. All the students talked about her. One was that her breath smelled like onions, which is why I never asked her a question after lunch. The other was that she picked her nose, which I didn't think was ladylike or appropriate for the public eyes. There were so many rumors out on that poor old lady that the last day of school, Alex had the nerves to ask Mrs. Kimberley if any of the rumors were true. Mrs. Kimberley whispered something in Alex's ear. Whatever she said made Alex walk back to his desk and he didn't say a work for the rest of the day.

After school, Nicole and me stopped by the coffee shop to buy our favorite homemade chocolate cookies. It was hard helping Nicole get through her breakup, which, I told her, would take time. She turned towards me while I was driving and said, "I wish I was as lucky as you."

"What do you mean?"

"You have a mother who loves you to death. My mom, I don't even know if she cares about me. I mean, she used to pretend to love me and my brothers, but now it's like she don't give a damn. And you have a good man. You don't ever have to worry about either one of them leaving your side."

"Nicole, I'm sure your mom still loves you, she's just going through some things."

"Well, she sure has a nice way of showing it, by drinking her life away."

"Well, my life is not as perfect as you think. My mom has always been too busy with her articles to talk to me. And Kenneth, he's leaving in a couple more days. I don't have clue where our relationship is going to end up. Whatever may happen, he knows that he will always have a place in my heart."

"I had no idea that Kenneth was leaving. You're taking this so well."

"Yeah." I said, but deep down inside I was hurting. I was the type of person who didn't like showing or expressing my feelings. No one knew how I felt about Kenneth, except him and me. And, I wanted to keep it that way, because as soon as you involve someone else in your relationship, you will hear a lot of "She say," "I heard," and "He said." Outsiders try to give you advice that they think you should take and will probably just make things worse. Then you'll wish that you would have listened to your heart.

But Nicole's heart was with Alex in that situation. Alex didn't love her the way that she loved him, so my suggestion for her would be to just move on and experience another heartbreak. Like my mom said, "Follow your first instincts, usually they're right."

"Snap out of it, Regina!" Nicole said, snapping her fingers in my face.

I looked at Nicole and said, "You better thank God you're a friend of mine because by now those fingers would have been broken."

"Whatever!" said Nicole, just about to walk out of the car, until she said, "Regina, how does it feel to be in love?"

I responded by saying, "I really can't explain it, but it's a wonderful feeling. I mean, you'll want to spend as much time as you can with each other, and you'll start getting butterflies in your stomach when that person is near." I said, smiling from ear to ear. "I could go on. It's something that I think everyone should experience in a lifetime. But don't worry, you will. It'll probably happen when you're least expecting it. You will just have to know or he might just pass you by. But enough of that! I'm on my way to see my man!"

As I arrived at Kenneth's house, I could see him on the riding mower. Maybe this is not a good time. He'll probably ask me to come by later. So, I started getting out of the car. Kenneth turned off the lawn mower, wiping sweat from his forehead. He said that his mom had him doing work around the house and maybe we could spend some time tomorrow.

"Tomorrow!" I said angrily. "Do you not realize that you will be leaving in a couple more days? Then, we won't be spending anytime together."

"Tomorrow, baby, I promise."

"Maybe you do realize it. Maybe you just don't care."

"Regina, it's not that I don't want to spend any time with you. I'm just tired."

"Being tired is not stopping us from laying in the bed together. I mean, I could give you a back massage and we could go to sleep together."

"Sounds great, Regina, but I'll pass. I have a whole lot of more housework to do."

"I could help."

"Thanks, but I can handle it."

I slowly walked back to my car. I could hear Kenneth saying, "I love you." I didn't bother looking or saying it back. I felt like I was losing him before he was even gone. Could this mean that our relationship was ending, or just me?

I went back home and sat on the couch next to my mom. I needed someone to talk to. This was the perfect opportunity for me to communicate with her. Usually, she's sitting on the couch with a briefcase, magazine, and a pen in her hand. So, I turned towards her and said, "So, have you thought about it?"

"About what?" my mom replied. "Have I thought about kicking you out? No, not yet."

I responded, "Well, whenever you think about that be sure to include some money." My mom grunted.

"Well, where would I go without money? Surely you're not going to kick me out on the streets."

"The only place that you need to go is with Kenneth."

"Kenneth is going to college and I'm going to beauty college here. I don't want to be the one standing in his way. I'd rather stay and wait on his return."

"So you're telling me, Mrs. Regina, that you're going to be sitting by the phone waiting on his calls for three years."

I really never thought about that. Would I really be waiting on his calls that long? I started walking upstairs to my bedroom. My mom knew just what to say to piss me off. I started thinking, *Should I go away with Kenneth, or just go on with my life until he returns?*

Kenneth called and told me that he wanted me to come over. We talked for hours. I told him about my mom trying to convince me to go away with him.

"That's what she wants and, of course, me. But is that what you want?"

"No," I responded. "I don't want to go with you. You're going be staying in a dorm. Where would I stay? I don't have enough money for a house. I mean, who knows how long it might take for me to get a job? I'll just stay and wait on you."

"Regina, is that what you plan on doing? You're a very attractive woman, who damn sure don't deserve to be alone. And I can just bet you that there's a guy out there waiting to take my place. When I'm finally gone, he'll probably approach you."

"Hate to tell you, but guys approach me now. Some of them don't care."

" I'm talking about the respectful ones."

"Kenneth, do you not plan on making our relationship work?"

"I'm sorry baby, but most long distance relationships don't work."

I jumped out of Kenneth's bed.

"You could at least have faith in us. We can prove to people that it is still possible. Kenneth, tell me if I'm wrong, because I'm coming to the conclusion that you don't want to be with me when you're gone."

"That's the thing, Regina. When I'm gone, we're not going to be together for a long time. I mean you know that I love you and I do plan on spending the rest of my life with you. Right now, I'm just confused." Kenneth said, popping his knuckles.

"What, exactly, are you confused about?"

"About us. I mean you say that you love me. Prove it. Move away with me."

"It's not that simple. I'm not going to stand here and let you and my mom pressure me into something that you two think I should do. I won't move away with you to prove a point. I never once have asked you to prove your love to me. I can't even believe that you did. We have been together for three years, so I really do believe that's enough proof."

"Regina, you took what I said the wrong way."

"Maybe I did."

Kenneth walked up to me and said, "I never meant to hurt you, but I meant half of everything that I said. I'm just trying to be the best man that I can be, by being with you." He lifted my chin with his hand, saying, "I wish I could read your mind. Please, tell me what you're thinking."

"If you really want to know, I'm thinking about walking out that door and not ever looking back." I pushed Kenneth's hand away, saying, "Remember when you said that you couldn't live without me? Well, it looks like you'll be living up north without me."

I just left afterwards. I don't know what had come over me. I was afraid of losing Kenneth. I didn't know how to act, since it was getting closer and closer for him to leave. As I arrived home I could see my mom sitting on the porch swing. I could just imagine why she was sitting outside. Kenneth had called her and told her everything. That was also one of the things I was mad about. Kenneth was always inviting my mom into our relationship. I stayed in the car for a while. I wasn't going to hear the last of it, might as well be prepared. Here it goes.

"Regina, what is wrong with you? Didn't I raise you to treat a good man better than that? You don't find too many men like Kenneth around. I guess you would rather have the type that forgets your b-day. The type that lies constantly. The type with no job or car. Or better yet, the one that can't do nothing for you, he's looking for someone to take care of him."

"Exactly who is that, Mom?"

"A no good man. Your friend Nicole has been through a lot of them, and me too. I went through a lot of good for nothing men before I met your daddy. Lord knows that he was the best thing that entered into my life. And he was taken away, just like that. He was good to me. I haven't been that happy with a man since. All I'm saying is, realize what you have before it's gone."

I just sat on the couch, listening to what she had to say, although it was going through one ear and out the other one. Was I actually being so selfish that I was letting Kenneth get away? I loved him, and I really wanted to be with him. I was graduating the same day that he leaves, so I could still manage to leave with him.

I turned towards my mom and said "I hope you're happy, because I have decided to leave with Kenneth."

My mom started smiling, saying, "Well, I hope it's not by anything I said."

"Of course not. I love him, and I know one day we will be married."

"Well, don't stand there and talk to me about it! Go call him!"

As I ran upstairs with excitement, the phone started ringing just as I was about to pick it up. "Whoa!" I said. "We have a very strong connection!" He knew that I would come around. I inhaled, then exhaled. "Yes, I'll go with you, and I'm just sorry about anything that I said earlier. I'm sorry, just let me know that you still love me."

"Hello! This is Nicole. Were you planning on leaving without telling me?"

"No, I just made this decision a couple minutes ago."

"I have some bad news."

"What is it? Is it about Kenneth?"

"No, it's about me." Nicole said in a sad voice.

"It can't possibly be that bad."

"I'm pregnant."

"You're what?"

"I'm pregnant, Regina. My whole life is over."

"No, don't say that. This is a new beginning for you. Your life has just begun. Have you told Alex?"

"No, I'm going to wait."

"Wait? Until when?"

"Graduation Day," Nicole said.

"Oh, no! The longer you wait, the more he'll think it's not his child. And you know how Alex is. He can be an asshole at times. So, it's best that I come pick you up and we go over to his house. I'm on my way." I said, hanging up the phone.

When Nicole and me arrived at Alex's house, we saw him sitting on the porch with the biggest whore in town, Shebba.

"He never loved me, and I don't even think he ever cared about me."

"Shut it up, Nicole. Now is not the time to be whining over his no good ass. It's not about you anymore, it's about your baby."

As we walked up to Alex, I demanded Shebba to leave. Shebba said, "Whatever you have to say to my man, you can say in front of me."

"This has nothing to do with you or me, so let's go for a walk and talk."

Shebba stood up, looking at Nicole, and said, "You better not be trying to make the moves on my man while I'm gone. I will be watching you."

"Watching me?" she said. "He was my man first! You took him from me. So you're the one who needs to be watched." Nicole said, upset. "Besides, I wouldn't waste my time on a second time with him."

"Then why are you here?" Shebba said, brushing her bang back.

"I'm here to announce that I'm pregnant."

"By who? Surely you're not trying to say Alex is the baby's daddy!"

"Alex IS the daddy and he's not going to deny this child, right Alex?"

"I don't remember having sex with you."

When Alex said that, I had to put my two cents in.

"Alex, do you not remember me walking in on you two having sex? I bet you'll remember when the baby is born and the DNA test will prove that it's yours!"

I was so mad that I got in the car with Nicole and took off, spinning. "Don't even worry about him Nicole, because as long as we have been friends, you know I have always been there for you. So don't think for a second that I would let you go through this alone. No matter how bad things get, just remember to keep your head up."

"He told me after we made love if I became pregnant that he would be there for me, no matter what. A guy will say anything just to continue to sleep with you. So, he just used me and filled my head up with his lies."

"Only because you let him, and you listened to him. It was lie after lie. You should have dumped him on Valentine's Day when he didn't bother to call or bring you anything. I thought that you may have seen the light for sure. But you continued to be in the dark."

Nicole started crying, "Why me? Why does my life have to be so bad? Can't I at least be happy, just once in my life?"

As bad as I wanted to go with Kenneth, I decided to stay and help Nicole out, so I never even bothered to call Kenneth that night. As days went by, I ignored Kenneth's calls.

It was finally graduation day. It seems like when you don't want a day to come, it arrives quicker than you can think. My mom was a little disappointed in the decision I had made. She said I shouldn't have to pay for Nicole's mistakes. I tried explaining to her that Nicole never asked me to stay. I'm staying because I want to. My mom was just going to have to get over it.

As I was putting my graduation gown on, I stared at the necklace on the table that Kenneth gave to me. He was leaving me with so many memories. Today was my graduation. I thought I was supposed to be happy, instead I was sad. I went to pick Nicole up. She handed me a letter that said:

To: Regina

From: Kenneth

I'm on my way to a far, far place and I hope that you will never forget my face. You are my diamond. Together, we will always shine. Apart, I will always keep you in mind. I love you now, and I'll love you tomorrow, until it becomes forever.

Love,
Kenneth

I was so happy to hear from him, even if it was just through a letter. "Where is he?" I said, looking at Nicole.

"I don't know. He didn't say where he was going."

I called his mom's house. She said that he was at the bus stop.

"Go to the bus stop!" Nicole said.

"No, I know that Kenneth wouldn't miss my graduation."

So, we went to my graduation. Just as I was making my speech, there Kenneth was, the love of my life. I let him know that I still loved him, in front of hundreds of people. Afterwards, we ran to each other with hugs and kisses.

Chapter Two

One year later I was living in my very own apartment, but not alone. My best friend and her baby, Lil Tracey, moved in with me. I loved helping her take care of her little baby. I even thought about having my own one day, although first I'll have to find a man. Alex didn't deny Lil Tracey, but he might as well have. All that he had to offer was himself. He was going to have to offer more than his love. He said that he wasn't giving Nicole any money because she would just spend it on herself.

Kenneth and I decided to go our separate ways. It was hard for me at first but I managed to live without him. So far, none of my dreams had come true. Kenneth had vanished out of my life, and having my very own beauty salon was completely out of the question, at least for now. Most of the time, I would stay home and baby-sit Lil Tracey while Nicole went out with her new guy friend, Michael.

My mom would come over sometimes. I would see her shaking her head. I guess she expected me to leave Nicole and her baby on the streets. She just seemed disappointed with me for putting my dreams on hold. So, she volunteered to help me get my very own beauty salon, but only if I agreed to pay half of it.

After my mom left, I laid on the couch with Lil Tracey in my arms. While watching show after show, I slowly fell asleep. Kenneth slowly picked me up and put me in bed. I opened my eyes. "You came back for me! I always knew that you would!" I was so excited that I jumped up and hugged him. We laughed and talked together.

I laughed so hard that I woke myself up. I could hear Kenneth's and my favorite song, "You Got It Bad" by Usher, playing on Midnight Love. I felt like I was being haunted by love, in some kind of way. I threw some water over my face. I could hear Nicole coming in from a good night with Michael. She left him with a good night kiss.

Afterwards, she sat on the couch talking to me about her good night out. She looked at me, saying, "What is that dripping from your face, water or sweat?"

"It's sweat," I said.

"Well, it's not hot in here," Nicole responded.

"I think that I'm coming down with something."

"A lot of people get love-sick," Nicole said. "Regina, are you still having dreams about Kenneth?" Nicole grabbed me a bag of ice and held it over my forehead. "You know that the only thing that is going to help you get over Kenneth is by moving on. For starters, Michael has a friend who wants to meet you."

"When?"

"Tomorrow night."

"I'm not interested." I just wasn't ready to meet anyone right then, but I knew I wasn't going to get over Kenneth any other way, so I agreed to meet Michael's friend.

"But only as a friend."

"No 'buts', Regina. If he's sweet to you, then let him be more. Besides I really do think that you will like him."

The next day, Nicole and me went shopping for something nice for me to wear. I was sort of happy to be going out. Wondering, would he be a jerk, a wannabe player, a pimp, or a Mack daddy. All I knew is that I was going to have fun that night, but without Kenneth.

"Nicole, I don't think that I'm ready for this."

"Don't bail on me now, I have gotten you this far."

"Since Kenneth gone, I feel as if my love for him has grown stronger than ever. Like they say, you never realize what you had until it's gone. How could I have let him get away?"

"Regina! Stop it! Stop doing this to yourself! You look a mess, and I'm the blame for it. That's why I'm trying to make it up, by getting you to go out with Michael's friend. Trust me, you won't regret this."

As we were walking and talking down the aisle, I could see Nicole's baby's daddy Alex with Shebba. Nicole pretended not to see them until we got in the checkout line behind them. Nicole picked up all Lil Tracey's items and threw them in Alex and Shebba's shopping cart.

"Excuse me, but who is going to pay for this?"

"Well, of course Alex," Nicole said, with an attitude.

Shebba rolled her eyes and said, and stated that Alex didn't have any money. "Probably because you took it all," Nicole said. There they were, arguing right in the store and that was soon going to lead us to getting kicked out of the store. All Alex did was grin from ear to ear. Since he seemed to think that it was all so funny, I convinced Nicole to put him on child support.

Afterwards, we started getting ready for our dates. I sat on the couch after I was done, impatiently waiting for Michael's friend to arrive. "Relax," Nicole said. "He'll be here in a minute." I was just ready to get this over with. Finally, there was a knock on the door. Nicole rushed to open it, hugging all over Michael. Behind him was a tall, light-skinned, and sexy guy with a rose in his hand. He walked next to me, handing me the rose. *Well, where's the rest of them*, I thought. He slowly moved his big, wet lips to say "Hi, I'm Jerome." I was speechless. I couldn't help but stare.

Finally, I introduced myself, with shyness. Jerome said, "You look even more beautiful than they described."

"You don't look so bad yourself." We just continued to stare at each other like we were about to attack one another.

"I guess that's what you two are going to be doing for the rest of the night. I mean, maybe you two should just give each other a picture, it will last longer."

Jerome said, "I'm here to show Regina a good time, and I'm going to start by taking her out to eat."

We went out to eat and he took me to a dance. Jerome put his arms around my waist and kissed me on the forehead. I laid my head on his shoulder. I felt safe in his arms, and like I had known him forever. Although, it felt quite different than when I was in Kenneth's arms. I don't think I will ever find a love like the one before. I didn't want to imagine what this was leading to, so I pushed Jerome away and backed off.

"Where is this leading to?" I asked.

He walked up to me, saying, "Wherever you want it to lead to."

"Just as friends."

"Then friends it is," Jerome said in a sexy tone.

We went back to my place and watched a movie. Jerome wanted to know a little bit more about me. As I talked, he sat there and listened. I couldn't believe he didn't fall asleep, and that he was so interested in my life. He also talked about himself, about how he used to be a dog and how he lost the only woman he loved by playing games. He said that he had been single for one year.

"If you loved her so much then how come you haven't tried to get her back?"

"If I could, then I would. But it's too late. She's gone."

"Gone where?" I asked.

"She's dead," Jerome said. "And it's my fault." A tear dropped from his eye.

"I'm so sorry, Jerome." I never really had a guy get emotional around me. Most guys try to hide their feelings and their tears. But it kind of turned me on, until he finished his story. He said his ex-committed suicide, from his games. I was a little shook up from his story. I looked at him, saying, "I'm not trying to be mean or anything, but some of us have to be shown the hard way. Just to make us realize our mistakes." I laid my head on his lap and he gently massaged my neck, which helped me release some stress off my shoulders.

By the time we focused back on the movie, it was going off. Michael and Nicole were walking in. "So what was the movie about?" Nicole asked. We both shrugged our shoulders, saying, "I don't know." "Hmmm," Nicole said, sucking on a lollipop. "It seems like they were having a little more fun than us, Michael." Nicole always seems to keep her mind in the gutter. Maybe that's why she had Lil Tracey— from curiosity.

"If you must know, we were getting more acquainted."

"In what kind of way?" Nicole asked, laughing.

Jerome gave me a goodbye kiss on the cheeks and said, "I had a really good time. I hope that you enjoyed tonight as much as me. Maybe we can do this again, real soon."

"Of course," I said, smiling.

After Jerome and Michael left, Nicole sat on the couch next to me with a bowl of ice cream. Just as I was about to head to my bedroom, Nicole said "Not so fast!"

"So, tell me," she said, stuffing ice cream into her mouth, "did you like him?"

"He was OK," I responded. "He just doesn't seem like boyfriend material. I mean, I see him more as a friend, like someone to talk to about my problems."

"Well, what's wrong with having him as your man to talk to?" Nicole said.

"I'm just not interested in him in that kind of way."

"So, you're telling me that you wouldn't go on another date with him?"

"You're absolutely right."

"What's wrong with him?"

"Nothing, Nicole. He's perfect." *A little too perfect*, I thought.

"I don't understand, Regina. I give you a date with the most handsome man around and you don't want to go out with him again." Here we go again, another night of Nicole's love preaching. "Regina, you're single and Jerome is single.

You two make a perfect match. No one wants to be alone and I don't see why you should be."

Maybe I was afraid to give my heart away once again to a man who would make promises to be with me forever and let nothing split us apart. How was I supposed to know whether he just wanted to enter my life and walk out of it, just like that? All I knew is that I wasn't ready for a relationship right now.

Suddenly, the phone started ringing. It was my mom, telling me about our family reunion in three weeks. Afterwards, I went to bed. The next morning, I saw Michael outside Nicole's door, with some bags aside him. *Nicole's going washing awfully early. I should get her to wash my shoes.*

"What's going on?" I asked, as I saw Nicole brushing her things into a bag.

"I'm moving in with Michael," she responded.

"Don't you think it's too soon?"

Nicole mumbled, "The sooner, the better."

"What's wrong, Nicole? Are you mad at me? Was it something I done?"

"Questions, questions, questions," Nicole said. "The question you should have been asking is 'When was me and my child going to let you breathe'?"

"That does not matter. You and your child give me my space. I enjoyed the company. Have you thought about this?"

"Yes," Nicole said, brushing her hair back. I have been thinking about this for quite awhile. I just never told you."

"Why?"

"Because Regina, you always try to make my decisions for me."

"You're so wrong, Nicole. I just gave you advice, which you could take or leave."

Nicole was acting quite strange. What had come over her? I couldn't believe the way that she was reacting. Nicole walked by me, grabbing her very last bag, saying, "I'm sorry if I'm sounding harsh. But I don't want me and my child to be a burden on you anymore." Nicole's eyes became watery.

She just continued talking, saying, "If it wasn't for me, you would probably be happily married to Kenneth. You see, I have made your life miserable and I don't want to ruin in any longer." There, Nicole was blaming herself for me not leaving with Kenneth. Nicole's last words were, "I'm going to make it up to you, some way, somehow, and someday."

After Nicole left, I started walking up and down the hallway thinking what I was going to do next. This was the perfect time to find a roommate, with no strings attached, so I could save up money for my own beauty salon. I grabbed the newspaper off the counter and looked through it. Still no luck. So I decided to post an ad in the newspaper. I even asked my mom if she knew anyone that was looking for a roommate. She said, "As a matter of fact, I do know someone. My best friend's son."

"A guy, mom?"

"What's the difference? A roommate is a roommate. By the way, have you heard from your friend, Nicole?" I shook my head no.

"See, she found love and happiness. Did she stay and help you out with your beauty salon? Of course not. I bet that didn't even cross her mind. Now you're here, alone with the decision you made."

"I never asked Nicole to stay and help me out. She doesn't have much. Besides, she has a baby to care for." I could never see myself taking or asking for a dime from her. I was so tired of my mom blaming Nicole, just because I decided to be alone.

Tomorrow was the family reunion and I was exhausted. My mom's best friend and son were going to be there. I gave my mom a kiss on the cheeks and went to work. I worked at a small convenience store. Nicole gave me a call at work, breaking the news that Shebba broke up with Alex.

"I wonder why?" I asked.

"Probably because he's paying child support for Lil Tracey and there's not enough money left for her!" We both started laughing. I was so happy for Nicole and her baby.

As I continued talking on the phone, I heard a deep voice say, "I didn't know that you worked here." I looked up but I really couldn't see who it was because the guy had a cap on, covering his eyes.

"Excuse me, do I know you?"

"It depends," he said. "Do you want to know me?"

"Well, I would like to know who I'm speaking with." He slowly removed his cap and looked up. My eyes began to get big. I still had Nicole on the phone. "Did you tell him where I worked?"

"Who?" Nicole asked. "Is Jerome there?"

"Yes."

"I told you that you two were meant to be. Otherwise, he wouldn't have found you like that. I'll talk to you later."

As I hung up and handed Jerome his change, he grabbed my hand, saying, "Don't be afraid. I won't hurt you. I just want to love you." He kissed my hand and I jerked it away, saying, "Goodbye, have a nice day and come back again." While leaving, he said, "Oh, I will. Maybe sometime today." Jerome was so out of his league. "That's something we have to say to all customers," I said to my co-worker.

After getting off work, I could see Jerome parked outside the store. "May I help you?" I said. "Take a picture, it might last longer."

"Can't you see how we meet up?" Jerome said. "Don't you think it was meant to be?"

"No," I said, getting in my car and taking off. I could see Jerome's car from a distance, still in the parking lot. I thought to myself, *just as long as he's not following me.*

The next morning, I awoke holding my favorite teddy bear that Kenneth gave me. It had his cologne all over it. While getting out of bed, I opened the door to check the mailbox. There on the porch was a bouquet of roses, addressed to me from Jerome. *This guy is crazy and romantic. That's definitely not a good combination. Add it up and it equals to obsessed. I'm surprised he doesn't have my phone number.* Just as I thought that, the phone began to ring. Maybe I was wrong.

I answered it and it was my mom. She wanted me to come over to help her set up stuff for the family reunion. As I arrived at my mom's house, I told her about Jerome, how he sent me roses and came to my job. I felt like I was being stalked. She advised for me to get a security alarm in my house, and some pepper spray. "And, please be careful," she said. "Because there are a lot of crazy people out there. You just never know who they are."

My mom's best friend was coming over to help out, which I was looking forward to meeting her son. I went to go look for a pitcher to make some Kool-Aid. The doorbell started ringing. While I was fixing some Kool-Aid, I heard that deep, sexy voice again, saying, "I told you that we were meant to be." I looked, and there stood Jerome. I threw the whole pitcher at him, yelling, "It's him!"

My mom came rushing in there. "It's who?" she asked.

"Jerome. He's the one that has been stalking me."

"Poor Jerome wouldn't harm anyone. He's my best friend's son!"

Jerome said "Since Regina seems to tell you everything, has she told you that I have taken her on a date? And we had a really good time, as I can recall."

"Regina didn't tell me anything. Come on in here later on and tell me more."

As my mom went back into the living room, I looked at Jerome and said, "So you were the one looking for a roommate?"

"Yeah, and you were the one needing a roommate."

"Let's get that part clear—I don't need anything, I just want."

"Huh," Jerome said. "What you need is a man. Maybe you wouldn't be so mean."

I grabbed a towel, continuing to argue with Jerome. "Who are you to tell me what I need?"

We just argued and argued. Afterwards, we just looked at each other and laughed.

"Do you think that I'm attractive?" Jerome said.

"You look OK." The truth was, he was fine but it's never good to tell a person that they're fine all the time. Especially if they're stuck on their self, because they might think they're too good to be with you. Or they might think that they're so fine that they can be with you and someone else.

I always seemed to get nervous around Jerome? What could it be? That I was falling for him, and that I wanted him as much as he wanted me? Of course not. I was still in love with Kenneth.

Jerome helped me clean up my mess. After I finished, I went to the bathroom and wet a towel to put over my face. You can just guess who followed me.

"Damn! Do I make you that hot? Would you like me to cool you down?"

"No, it's not that. I'm just not feeling well."

"Well, all you need is some medicine and I'll be more than happy to prescribe it to you." Jerome grabbed my hand as I tried leaving. "I'm not letting you get away that easily."

"What do you want, Jerome? What do you want me as?"

"I want you as my queen, my baby, my freak, and especially as my woman. So, can I have you as one of them?"

"You could have me as all of them, if you were my man. But you're not."

I looked at him, in the eyes, wondering if I could read his mind. Although it seemed as if he was reading my mind. I was definitely falling for him, but I was afraid, afraid of being loved by someone other than Kenneth. Like before, I pushed him away again. I went outside and took a picture of Kenneth and me out of my back pocket. Every day I had been wishing and praying that he would come back to me. I said aloud, "Just maybe it is time to move on."

"Maybe it is time to move on, with me." Jerome said, standing behind me.

Chapter Three

My mom convinced me to let Jerome move in with me, but I only let him move in as a roommate. The next day, Jerome and his friends started moving some of his things in. Jerome was staring at me so hard that he dropped the TV on his foot. Ouch! That had to of hurt! So, I ran to see if he was all right. He just stood there, whining like a baby while all his friends were laughing at him, saying, "Love hurts!"

I helped Jerome to the couch and he hopped all the way there on one foot. I grabbed a bag of ice and put it on his hurt foot. I was concerned about him, so I begged for him to go to the emergency room because it could be broken. His guy friends still seemed to think it was funny, yelling out, "Playa! Playa!" Was this all a joke? He looked hurt to me. I saw the TV drop, but I didn't know if it dropped on his foot or not. Could he have been playing' me, just to get next to me? Whatever was going on, I was going to get to the bottom of this.

I went to my room, thinking, *what have I gotten myself into? Why did I agree to let Jerome move in?* Now that I have a roommate, people are calling 24/7. They seemed to notice my ad in the newspaper. I went back in the living room to explain to Jerome that we could never be more than friends. I didn't want to dis him in front of his friends, but he gave me no choice. He would just continue this false allegation.

As I stood up with my hands on my hips and a frown on my face, Jerome said, "What's wrong with you?"

"What's wrong with me? Jerome, you seem to think that you and me are a pair."

"A brother's foot is broken and all you want to do is argue. If it makes you happy, I'll leave you alone."

Jerome jumped up off the couch and left with his boys. I had a feeling he was playing games. I sat on the couch, watching TV, waiting for Jerome to come in. I really was starting to like him. I mean, if he did all of this to get my attention, he can't be that bad of a man. I guess I was playing hard to get. Tonight, when he comes in, I'm going to tell him how I really feel about him. Besides, I think it's about time that I move on. I'm sure Kenneth would understand. He's probably moved on, also.

I went and put on a red sexy gown and sprayed my favorite perfume on my neck, imagining Jerome sniffing and kissing there. Just as I heard the door shut, I walked out of the bedroom with a big smile on my face that quickly turned to a frown. There stood Jerome, and he wasn't alone. He had a woman with him, heading straight to his bedroom!

I was a little disappointed. Hell! I was mad! Jerome walked into the kitchen with his shirt off and boxers on. He looked at me and said, "Are you expecting someone?" Little did he know I was expecting him, but not with another woman. He was probably doing this to make me mad, and boy, did it work!

"Jerome, is that your girlfriend?"

"No," he responded. She's just someone that I picked up at the club."

He poured two glasses of champagne in my expensive glasses and said, "Who's the lucky man?"

"What makes you think that he's lucky?" I asked.

"Because, look at you. You look beautiful. And I love the candles and everything. Well, don't mind me, I'll be in my bedroom."

As I watched Jerome walk off, I wanted to grab him and tell him that he was that lucky man, but I just let him go. I wanted to knock the door down. That's supposed to be me in there, having a good time with him! I couldn't believe this. I went to my bedroom and slammed the door. A couple of minutes later, I could hear them moaning and grinding, and the girl from the club screaming Jerome's name.

I grabbed my keys off the dresser and took a long drive. I didn't know where I was going, just as long as I wasn't there. Well, I ended up at my mom's house. She was working on an article. I went up to my old bedroom, staring out my window at the stars in the sky. I saw a falling star, so I made a quick wish and laid on my bed and fell asleep.

The next morning, I went back home. Just as I was stepping out of my car, I saw Jerome and the girl from the club leaving the apartment, kissing all over each other as if they fell in love overnight. We walked past each other without saying a word. *I guess he'll never know how I feel about him.* I opened my apartment door, taking one last look back. I could see Jerome all over the girl from the club. He pretended not to see me, but I know that he saw me.

I went to work mad and when I came home, I was even madder. Jerome and the girl were lying on my new couch, and he knew that I didn't allow that. I explained that to him when he was moving in. What was it going to be next? Was he going to have the girl in my lingerie, cooking for his ass? I couldn't even think straight; all I could do was scream.

They both jumped up like just got caught having sex by their parents. "What's wrong?" Jerome asked.

"You were lying on my new couch! Hello!"

His girlfriend just stood there, rolling her eyes. I wanted to punch her in the forehead to make her eyes stay in place, but that wouldn't have been nice. So, I went up to my bedroom and took a nap.

After waking up, I slowly dragged my feet to the bathroom. As I opened the door, I could see Jerome stepping out of the shower. Just as I was about to hand him the towel and help dry him off, Jerome's girlfriend walked in, saying, "What are you doing here? I'll take that!" I stepped outside the bathroom door, staring at Jerome until she slammed the door in my face. I kind of think he enjoyed me walking in on him. I have to admit, I did.

I could hear Nicole, singing her way up to my apartment. I ran outside to tell her what had happened. We walked back into my apartment. Jerome and his girl were watching TV. I think she was pissed off, because she grabbed her keys, and Jerome, and took off.

"That's just how it is when you have more than one person living with you and there's only one bathroom. There are going to be surprises and unexpected things happening."

Nicole had grown up a lot from high school. I couldn't believe that she was giving me advice that I was willing to listen to. She also announced that she was engaged. And here I was, I was single.

I told Nicole that I liked Jerome a lot, and that I missed the attention that he was giving me. "Now he's not giving me any attention at all, since she came along."

"It's not too late, Regina. He's not married yet."

"Well, I know that's not going to happen anytime soon."

"Anything is possible," Nicole said. "Just let him know how you feel, before it's too late."

After Nicole left, I waited on Jerome to come home but he never returned until the next morning. I didn't really know how to explain the way that I was starting to feel about him. Watching the way that he treated his new girlfriend made me realize that he was a good man, and not out to play me.

But that was a chance at the time that I wasn't willing to take. I had to find out with him being with someone else. But, just because her treated her like a queen didn't mean he would treat me the same. All of a sudden, I started having mixed feelings about him. Although we were living together, I still didn't know him quite well.

I knocked on his bedroom door. He told me to come in. I was just about to tell him how I felt, until I saw suitcases on his bed. "Where are you going?" I asked.

"I'm going to live with my girlfriend," Jerome replied.

"You don't even know her that well."

"I didn't know you, but I moved in with you."

"But that's different. We are just roommates."

"I love her. She's my world. Every little thing she does amazes me. I don't think there's another woman out there quite like her."

How could he possibly be in love with her so fast? He definitely has love confused with lust. "Well, I guess what I have to say won't matter," I said, upset.

"What's on your mind?" Jerome asked.

"I was just thinking about asking you if you would like to go out for a bite to eat."

"That's the least I can do," Jerome said.

I left his room. What was I thinking by asking to go out for a bite to eat? I wanted to ask him if he would like to go out with me. Like, as his girl. He'll never know how I felt if I keep this up.

Later on, we went out for pizza. I was stuffed and crushed. All Jerome talked about was his girlfriend. I didn't want to hear that. I wanted him to talk about the two of us. Suddenly, he asked, "How are you and your new man?"

"Oh! It didn't work out. He blew me off that night that I was waiting on him. He dissed me for another woman."

"What's his name?" Jerome asked. I sat there biting my on lip, until I saw Kenneth's mom walking over, saying, "Kenneth talks about you every time he calls. He told me if I see you around to tell you that he still loves you." After she left Jerome said, "So his name is Kenneth." "Yeah!" I said.

"How can he possibly love you by doing you like that?"

"You don't know shit about him! How dare you say that he doesn't love me!"

"I just think you should find another man."

"Like who, Jerome? You?"

How dare Jerome sit there and try to make Kenneth out to be a bad person. I wanted to break down in tears. I guess I made Jerome think that it was Kenneth; that was my fault. I left Jerome eating pizza alone. Why stay? He wasn't my man. He was someone else's, and that seemed to make me want him even more. I went to the store to buy a newspaper to find a roommate, like before. Still no luck.

I was going to have my very own salon, one way or the other. I called my mom and she told me some good news, which was that she found a salon for sale and that she would pay for it. So, we went and took a look at it. "This is perfect!" I said. My mom bought the salon for me and said, "Don't ever say I haven't done anything for you." I was so excited that I stayed there all night. I didn't have a reason to go home. The next morning, I saw Jerome delivering mail, so I ran outside, waiting on him to come by.

"Is this you?" Jerome asked.

"Yes, this is me!" I said, smiling.

"I'm happy for you," Jerome said. "Maybe now you'll stop looking mad at the world."

I stayed happy for a while. One night, I even called Nicole to go out with me to the club, but she was tied down with Lil Tracey. I didn't know what to do to have a good time, so I just went over to Nicole's house. She was mad at me because I didn't tell Jerome how I felt about him.

"I don't think that it would have changed anything. Besides, I didn't have time to explain how I felt about him because he told me first how he feels."

"About you?" Nicole asked.

"No! About his girlfriend!"

"There has to be someone to hook you up with."

"Don't just find me anyone. I deserve someone who's smart, funny and fine, like me."

"Don't flatter yourself, Regina, because you don't usually get what you ask for. Everyone gets a chance to be loved and hurt. Some people get hurt over and over again. What I'm trying to say is, true love is hard to find."

"Maybe it will find me!" I said, laughing.

"No relationship is going to be perfect and there are going to be ups and downs. Whether you're ready for it or not, life is not perfect and neither are you."

"Nicole, maybe you should try getting your own talk show. Or being a love counselor, or something. People will actually pay and listen to you."

"Well, I do love to listen to people's problems in their relationships."

Nicole continued giving me advice and I listened. Finally, I went home to a good night's sleep.

Chapter Four

One month later. Working at my salon has been great. My number one customer is my best friend's enemy, Shebba. She comes by to get her hair done every weekend, and she doesn't even have a job. I guess some people just got it like that.

Jerome was calling me all the time, asking me for advice on his relationship. He seemed to think his girlfriend was cheating on him. I just wanted to lie and say she was, so he would come running to me. But I told him I didn't have clue. I just told him to ask her. "I've already done that," he said. "She just denies everything." I didn't know what to say to him. From everything that he'd told me, I was just as confused as him.

After I got off work, Jerome and me went to the park. I thought that he needed a shoulder to lean on, and mine was available. I really didn't know if now was the time to express my feelings or not. It was better now than never. It wasn't about her any longer. It was about me. She messed up her chance, now it was my turn to smile.

After I told him, he said that he wasn't going back home, so I offered him to move back in with me. He didn't turn the offer down. Every other day, Jerome would come to my shop with flowers. He was so romantic and sweet. I couldn't have asked more. All my dreams had come true. I was no longer alone.

On Valentine's Day, Jerome and me made passionate love as the rain fell down my window. This was the most incredible feeling that I had felt in a while. I think that I was falling in love. I laid my head down on his chest and he told me how much he cared about me, and how he would never hurt me. He said all the things that a woman would want to hear.

Afterwards, we went to my salon to clean up, but Jerome just couldn't keep his eyes and hands off of me.

There was definitely love in the air when Regina and Jerome hooked up. Wherever you saw Regina, Jerome was either there or somewhere near. I had never felt so happy and love, except when I was with Kenneth. There were times that he would still cross my mind. Before I met Jerome, I was still living in the memories that Kenneth and me shared together, which seemed to have been the only thing that kept me going.

It's known that if you jump out of one relationship, don't expect things to be all good in the next one. I think Jerome left his girlfriend for all the right reasons. He didn't trust her, so therefore he didn't need to be with her. The life that I was living was just too good to be true. Maybe this is all a dream. A dream that I never wanted to wake up from.

Jerome wrapped his big arms around my waist, and we slow danced in my salon until Jerome's ex-girlfriend came banging on the window. I rushed to open the door. "I hope you're happy, and proud of yourself for splitting us up!" she said. "I could tell that you wanted him all along by the way that you looked at him, and you didn't like me. I wonder why? Maybe it's because I had something that you wanted. Well, congratulations! You have him now! At least when he was with me, he wasn't pretending to love me!"

Jerome rushed to the door, saying, "What are you doing here? Regina didn't have anything to do with us splitting up! It just wasn't meant to be."

"So, you and her are meant to be?" she said. "I hope you know that he's going to take your heart and burn it, just like he did mine. And always remember, what goes around comes around, twice as bad," she said, walking off.

"Jerome, what is she talking about when she said that 'at least he wasn't pretending to love me'?"

"Don't listen to her. She's crazy! She just wants me back, but it's not going to happen as long as I'm with you."

Was Jerome lying? Would he break his promise, when he said that he would never hurt me? I had waited so long before I had gotten involved with anyone. Maybe she *was* crazy. So crazy about Jerome that she was willing to do or say anything to get him back. There was no way that I was going to let her ruin my relationship with Jerome.

So, we continued being in love and promised not to let anything or anyone split us up. Afterwards, we went to the park, watching old and young couples pass by. We stayed at the park and watched the sun set.

I hadn't seen my best friend in a while. She had left numerous messages on my answer machine. I just never had the time to return them. I spent all my time working and with Jerome. Friday night, we went to the movies. I saw Nicole there. She said, "I haven't seen you in a while. Where have you been?" "I've been around," I responded. The truth was, I was in love and I didn't want to make the time to spend with friends. I wanted to spend every minute and second with Jerome.

We were going to see the same movie so Nicole sat beside me, talking about everything that was going on. Jerome suggested that we move to another seat. Nicole looked mad after we moved. I told Jerome that I hadn't seen her in a while and that she just had a lot to talk to me about. "We have our own life, we don't need to listen to other people's lives." He crossed his arms, saying, "You can go back over there if you want."

I know that he didn't mean it. I felt like my man was trying to make me choose between my friend and him. I chose to be by her side the first time, and I ended up losing the love of my life. No way was I going to do it again. I was happy and no one was going to ruin it, not even Nicole.

I walked to the bathroom and I could see Nicole getting out of her seat. Boy, was I going to hear an earful. Entering into the bathroom, I could see Nicole through the mirror. "Why are you following me?" I asked.

"What's wrong with you, Regina? Ever since you have been with Jerome, you have been acting weird towards your family and friends. I don't even hear from you anymore because you're so wrapped around Jerome. You can't even find time for your best friend and family."

"I have been thinking about dropping by," I said.

"Exactly when were you thinking about dropping by? When hell freezes over?"

I could see that Nicole was very upset, so I promised her that I would drop by this weekend. We gave each other a hug and returned back to our seats.

When Jerome and me returned home, he filled the bathtub with bubbles and lit candles beside the tub. Jerome said that he was going to a game this weekend, and that he wanted me to go. I said sure, not thinking that I promised Nicole that I would drop by her house. I thought Sunday would be good, until I arrived at work and saw my name on the schedule.

My friendship with Nicole was falling apart; it was turning into a complete disaster. So, I gave her a call, hoping that she would understand but she hung the phone up in my face. All I could hear was the dial tone.

A couple of hours later, Nicole dropped by my store and handed me the other half of our best friend's pendant. I guess our friendship was over. I wasn't going to try to make it work. I felt like she didn't want me to be happy in life without her being in it. Maybe one day she will realize that I have a life, just like her, and that I'm not always going to be around. I thought she was a true friend. I guess I was wrong. It seems that I never knew her at all. I was starting to have regrets from everything that I had done for her. From this day forward, I didn't care if I ever saw or heard from her again.

I tried talking to Jerome about Nicole and me. He just said, "If she can't respect that you have a man, then you don't need her as a friend. I want to be more than your friend." Jerome took a box out of his pocket. He opened the box, putting an engagement ring on my finger.

I was speechless. My throat all of a sudden became dry. I started sweating and my nose started running. My nerves were going out of control. "Water!" I said to Jerome.

He gave me a glass of water and said, "I thought you would be ready. If you're not, then I understand." I looked at him and said, "I'm ready! I just wasn't expecting this."

One year later, I was happily married. Until the wedding bands hit our fingers.

Chapter Five

Jerome started working all the time, leaving us less time to spend with each other. I would only see him when he would come in, after that he would go take a shower and go straight to bed. I assumed he was tired, so I let him sleep. I went to bed to cuddle up with him later on that night, but he just pushed me away. We slept in the same bed, but not next to each other. He lay on one side of the bed, and I slept on the other side. I just lay there, holding onto my pillow, wondering what was wrong with Jerome.

He had started working this new job, and all of a sudden, he changed. He would say how I had it easy since I owned a salon, and that I could come and go as I pleased. Although my job wasn't as hard as his job, I still worked and paid the majority of the bills. I don't understand why he was complaining about who worked the hardest, or who was bringing the most money home. I thought we were in this together, not alone.

I got out of bed and went into the living room for a while. Even though Jerome worked hard and was down, I was willing to stay by his side. I went back and lay down in bed. Jerome moved to my side of the bed and put his arms around me, saying, "Everything is going to be all right. I'm just going through a hard time at work. I'm sorry for taking my anger out on you. Let me make it up to you by having a picnic, at the park, on the ground."

The next day, we went to the park and ate, laughed, and talked. Afterwards, we played a little one-on-one basketball. Jerome won, saying, "May the best player win!" When we arrived home, he helped me with the dishes.

"You're being awfully nice," I said. "What's up your sleeve?"

"Can I borrow your car tonight, to see my boys?"

"I guess, since your car is in the shop."

Jerome left around 8 p.m. I went to bed an hour later and awoke at 2 a.m. I turned over in bed and realized Jerome was not there. Maybe he didn't want to wake me so he decided to sleep on the couch. I walked into the living room but there was no sign of Jerome. I was so angry that I started shaking when picking up the phone to call his cell.

"Where are you?" I asked. "Do you know what time it is?"

He paused for a minute and said, "It's 2 a.m. I'll be home in a second. I just lost track of time."

What was he doing to lose track of time? I wondered, holding the phone.

"I love you," he said.

"If you loved me the way that you say you do, you would be at home with me instead of out in the streets doing who knows what. I shouldn't have to wake up in the middle of the night alone, or call you to come home. You should know where your home is." I could hear loud music and girls laughing in the background.

"Who the hell is that?"

"Oh! That's my homeboy's girls. You can come kick it with us, if you want."

"The only thing I'm going to be kicking is my foot up your ass if you don't come home with my car! I'm giving you 20 minutes or I'm calling the cops and say it was stolen," I said in an angry tone, slamming the phone down.

The only thing that came to my mind was that he was messing around. What else was I supposed to think? I'm sure every woman would think the same. Jerome came home in 15 minutes. Just as he stepped in the house, I snatched my keys out of his hand and said, "Don't expect to borrow my car again! Wherever you need to go, you better call your so-called friends or walk on those two feet that God gave you!"

Jerome started walking to my bedroom. I ran to my bedroom door, saying, "This is no longer your bedroom! I suggest that you start making yourself comfortable on the couch!" Who knows who he had been screwing. All I know is that he wasn't lying on my clean sheets. He was dirty to me in so many ways.

Jerome stood outside my door, knocking and apologizing. I accepted his apology but he still wasn't getting in, to kiss me all over like everything was all right. We had been through this once before, but I was weak in the knees and let him in anyway.

"Regina! You know that I love you and I wouldn't do anything to hurt you intentionally. Cheating shouldn't even cross your mind, as long as you're with me. When I'm going out, I'm kicking it with my boys! You should come with me, sometime." Jerome's friends were not the type of crowd that I liked hanging around.

Later on, that morning, we made love. We ate breakfast together and talked. Later, I went to work. On my way to work, I saw Nicole. I tried stopping her but she just ignored me, like I was a stranger. What had I done so bad that Nicole didn't want anything to do with me? I decided not to open my shop today. I went to Nicole's house, waiting on her to come back home. When she arrived back home, she said, "I hope you know that you can get put in jail for stalking."

"I'm not stalking you, Nicole! I just want to talk to you."

Nicole rolled her eyes, saying, "Well, that's what you have Jerome for."

"Why are you blowing me off?"

"Regina! You need to open up your big brown eyes and realize you're the one that's blowing people off. But I guess you can't see that, because you're so stuck on Jerome, like paper on glue."

"I finally get a chance to love again, and everyone wants to turn against me!"

"I am happy for you, Regina. But I am not happy that you have betrayed your family and friends. By the way, when is the last time you have spoken to, or seen, your mom?" Nicole said, walking off.

"Why?" I said, walking behind her. "Has she asked about me?"

"Duh!" Nicole said. "What's wrong with you? She is your mom, the woman that gave you birth. Two days, and two nights, in labor with your ass. And, I've told her the way that you have been reacting. She says that you will come to your senses. I just hope you do, before it's too late."

I called my mom, but she wasn't there so I just left a message.

"Where's Lil Tracey?"

"She's with her daddy. He's keeping her all day."

"Are you two planning on getting back together?"

"No, I don't ever want to be with him again, after everything that he put me through. I just want him to be in his daughter's life. And he wants to do just that. I'm still with Michael. We are still engaged to be married."

I held out my hand, flashing my 24 karat gold wedding band.

"You're married?"

"Yeah," I said.

"So, how's the married life?"

"It's great," I responded.

"Most people say that things change when you get married. That's why I'm taking my time, to make sure that this is what Michael and me really want. But if you're happy, then I'm happy for you."

Things had really changed since me and Jerome got married. I wish I could start all over. I would have gotten to know Jerome a little better. But to me, it seems even if you have known someone for a long period of time, you still really don't know him or her. They can still shock you with surprises. All I can do now is try to make things work in my marriage. I didn't want to tell anyone that I believed my marriage was falling apart.

"Where is Jerome?" asked Nicole.

"He's at work."

"Isn't that where you should be?"

"No, I decided not to open my shop today. I thought today would be perfect to visit the people I love."

"I'm glad that you finally came around."

I handed Nicole back half of our best friends pendant. "I'm sorry for reacting the way that I have. I hope that you will find it in your heart to forgive me."

"Well, it seems like I already have. I mean I haven't kicked you out yet!"

After talking with Nicole, I went to go visit my mom. She said, "So how's things with you and your husband?"

"How did you know?"

"I'm your mother, and you should know by now that you can't get nothing past me."

We talked for hours. I went home around 9 p.m. Jerome was nowhere in sight, once again. So, I called him on his cell.

"Where have you been?" he said.

"I've been visiting my mom and Nicole."

"Why didn't you tell me?"

"I didn't know that I had to check in with you to visit with my family," I said.

"I was just worried. I'll be home in a bit," Jerome said, hanging up the phone.

When Jerome came home, he jumped in the shower, grabbed himself a bite to eat, and made himself comfortable on the couch. I tried sitting beside him, but he acted as if he didn't want me anywhere near him. So, I moved to the other couch and watched TV.

Finally, Jerome said, "You know there are a lot of rumors going on at my job about you."

"What kind of rumors?" I said.

"All kinds," Jerome said. But there is only one that I'm concerned about, which is cheating."

"What? Jerome, are you high, or drunk? You can't be serious!"

"Yes, I am. That was the word of the day, cheating."

"Who am I cheating on you with? My mom and Nicole?"

"Hmmm. You got jokes. No, it's a guy, Regina, don't play games."

"Well, let me guess," I said. "You believe this rumor. Well, of course, or you wouldn't have ever asked me that. I have never cheated on you, or even thought about it. Who said it, Jerome?"

Jerome didn't say a word. I don't believe he'd heard anything. He was just jealous of me spending time with someone other than him. What would make him say something like that? Maybe he was the one cheating, and I was too blind to see. If someone else was in my situation, I would be able to see what was going on, but since it's me, I'm in denial. Could Jerome's job be making him have mood swings like this, or another woman?

That night I lay in the bed alone, while Jerome slept on the couch. At this moment, I really needed someone to talk to, so I called Nicole. She said she hadn't heard anything. "Are you crying?" she asked.

"Yeah, it's this romance movie that I'm watching. What a happy ending."

"Whatever, Regina! I have been knowing you forever. Don't let Jerome bring you down. You don't need a man to be complete. I admired you a whole lot before you got with him. You are brilliant. You have dreams that you have made come true. And you saved up money for that. Afterwards, you went to beauty school and passed with flying colors. You pushed yourself and you never gave up. And that's why I admire you. You will get though this, one way or the other. Just don't cry," Nicole said.

I dried my tears and eventually went to sleep. The next morning, Jerome woke me up with breakfast in bed. I was still mad from last night, so I pushed it aside and got ready for work.

"Are you not hungry?" Jerome said.

"Yeah, I am. I just don't take food from strangers."

"I'm not a stranger! I'm your husband."

"I don't know who you are. I mean, last night it was 'My wife's cheating on me', now you're acting yourself. My husband would never accuse me of cheating."

"I'm sorry," he said.

"It's like you have a split personality, and I don't know how much longer that I can deal with this. I used to be a sweet, caring, and lovely wife. Having you a hot meal when you came from work. The bathtub filled with hot steaming water. And, when you were aching, I gave you a back massage. You name it and I done it. Now, I've become fed up!" I left for work.

When I arrived, I saw Shebba stepping into my salon with a black short mini skirt on. "Could you squeeze me in for tomorrow?" she asked.

"Sure."

"So, how's Jerome?"

"He's fine," I said.

"That, he is," Shebba said, walking out the door.

How does she know Jerome? I thought. *He's not even from around here.*

"He doesn't have to be from around here for Shebba to know him," one of my customers said. "You better watch her."

Everyone just started gossiping in the shop. So, I called Jerome.

"Do you know a girl named Shebba?" I asked.

"No, why? What did she say?"

"She thinks you're fine."

"I don't know her," he said.

"Maybe she will tell me how she knows you tomorrow."

"Go ahead and ask her."

"Jerome, you better not be having me up here, looking like your fool."

"What do you mean? You're my woman."

"Whatever! That's what you want me to think, that I'm your woman. But really, I'm your fool for believing you."

"You are my woman. My #1."

"By the way, what are you doing?"

"Thinking about you," he said.

We all know that Jerome hasn't been thinking about me for a while. I no longer wanted to hear his lies, so I hung up.

When I arrived home, Jerome had the lights turned down low, candles lit everywhere, and a bucket of ice on the table with my favorite champagne in it. He turned on some nice, slow music. Jerome's chest was filled with oil that left a nice shine. He danced his way towards me. As he began to move closer to me, I moved back. He moved even closer, grabbing my purse out of my hand, sitting it on the couch. "Tonight is all about me and you."

"Why can't every night and day be about us? What makes tonight so special?" I said.

"Every day is special when I'm with you."

"Well, I'm sorry but I'm not in a romantic mood. It's funny how most of you guys don't understand women. We don't understand ya'll. I mean, especially with the lies. Why can't you all just tell us the truth? Then, you wonder why we don't want to have sex. Treat us like a lady and then we would be more than glad to have sex. Otherwise, we will keep it on lock down for as long as we want. We do hold something that you all crave like a drug. And for us, we can go buy batteries, if you know what I mean." I went walking to my room and, of course, Jerome was walking right behind me.

"I thought this was what you wanted."

"Well, you thought wrong. What I want is you. I want you to spend more time with me, instead of always out in the streets with your boys. Is that too much to ask for?" I asked.

Jerome grabbed my hand, saying, "You know that I love you. I may not say it all the time, but I do."

"Actions speak louder than words, and you haven't even been showing it anymore."

Jerome constantly talked and talked, saying, "You mean the world to me. And, if there's anything that you need or want, I'll get it for you."

"That's the thing, Jerome. I don't want all of that material shit. Haven't you ever been told that money can't buy love?" No matter how much I tried explaining to Jerome, it seemed to go in one ear and out the other.

I had been having a strange feeling about Jerome cheating on me for a while. Why haven't I shoved him to the curb? Because I needed proof. Could the proof be right under my nose? Besides, why couldn't he be a man and tell me the truth? Was he looking for an easy way to tell me that he was cheating? No matter what, to admit that you're cheating, it couldn't be told in any easy way. All I could do was try to understand what lead him into this and move on with my life, which would leave me heartbroken again.

The next morning when I went to work, I waited on Shebba to walk through the door. I really wasn't for sure if I was ready to hear that Jerome was cheating on me with Shebba, or anyone. As much as I tried to have faith in our marriage, and faith in my man, I didn't. I just had to find out, no matter what. Here it goes. Shebba walked in and I took a deep breath.

"How are you today, Mrs. Regina?"

"OK," I said.

Shebba started describing the type of style she wanted. If she was messing around with Jerome, I was going to give her an unforgettable style. As I was combing Shebba's hair, I asked her how did she know Jerome? She said, "It's a long story."

"I have time to listen."

"Well, I met him at the grocery store. At the time, I didn't know that he was your man. He was a new face in town, and I just had to introduce myself and get to know him. He told me that his name was Jerome. I watched him put strawberries into his shopping cart. I noticed a wedding band on his finger, so I asked him who was the lucky girl? That's when he said your name, and that's how I know him."

"That does not mean that you know him! You met him one time, so you know him?"

I don't know if I was buying Shebba's story or not. It might have been true, but I believed there was more to it. Jerome had lied to me once again. He didn't tell me that they met in the grocery store.

"Have you two met since then?" I asked.

"What   do   you   mean?"

"Come on, Shebba, don't play with me! We are two grown women, and I think you know what I'm trying to say. If not, are you messing around with Jerome?"

"No, Regina! I just think he's fine! I have never messed with Jerome. Come on! He's married to you." Afterwards, Shebba started laughing and saying that I was crazy.

Jerome seemed to think that I was crazy, also. When I arrived home, I told Jerome Shebba's story. He said, "I can't remember everyone's name! Besides, I wouldn't touch her with a 10 ft pole! She looks like she gets around." We started laughing. We sat together on the couch, eating popcorn and talking about everyone else's relationship except our own.

When Jerome turned his head, I noticed a big red mark on his neck. "Is that a hickey on your neck, Jerome?" He just sat there, looking guilty. I went to my bedroom and packed me a bag. I couldn't believe this. Just when I thought things were getting better. Instead, they were getting worse. Tears began falling down my face. How could I be so stupid? All the signs were right there in my face. I felt like someone had ripped my heart out.

Jerome entered the room, saying, "I was going to tell you about this."

"When, Jerome? When were you going to tell me about the hickey, the late nights out, and the rest?"

"Baby! This is not a hickey! I got stung by a bee! You're exaggerating."

"Oh, really? I have gotten stung by you, and it hurts." I grabbed my bag and pushed Jerome out of the way. I looked back and said, "I'm sick and tired of your lies! Can't you see that I'm hurting because of you? But you don't care, so why should I?"

Chapter Six

I went to go check into a hotel. I lay down on my bed, wondering what I had done with my life. Here I was, all alone in a room. Was that what I was seeking? Freedom? Of course not. I lay there, thinking about when Jerome and me met. I wasn't interested at that point and sometimes I wish it would have stayed that way. Maybe we rushed into this marriage thing too quickly. I knew that I still loved Jerome, and that he still loved me. I just don't think he was ready to settle down.

I hope he doesn't think I'm going to commit suicide, like his ex. He's not worth me taking my life for. I was thinking all kind of crazy things, but suicide was not one. I wanted to trust Jerome, but I couldn't, although trust is one of the most important things that you need in a relationship.

I decided to go to the store to pick up some junk food and grab a book or movie. Although life doesn't always go like in a book or movie, you don't always live happily ever after together. When I walked into the store, I didn't want to talk to or see anyone that I knew. When I was leaving out of the store, I saw Nicole and her family. I tried putting my bags over my face, but that didn't work. Nicole yelled out my name, walking towards my car.

"What's wrong?" she asked. "Have you been crying?"

"No, it's my allergies. You know how bad they can get."

Nicole said, "Guess who's in town?

"Tyrese." I wished.

"Kenneth is in town, for two weeks. He talked about you for at least an hour, in this parking lot earlier today. He looked sort of sad when I told him you were married."

"Not for long," I said.

"What's wrong?"

"I think Jerome is cheating on me."

"Are you sure? Because you two look so happy together."

"Just because we look happy doesn't mean that we are. Nicole, I saw a hickey on Jerome's neck while I was kissing him."

"Oh my God, Regina! You should that know he's cheating! Well, sorry. Here's Kenneth's number that he wanted me to give to you."

I grabbed the number and said, "I don't want to talk to any guys right now. They're all dogs."

"No, they're not. You just chose the wrong one."

"Nicole, you're the one that suggested for me to date him."

"True, but I didn't tell you to marry him."

After talking with Nicole, I went back to the hotel. I sat down on the couch with a bowl of ice cream that I didn't even feel like eating. So, I jumped in the shower, and broke down in tears. While getting out of the shower, I could hear someone knocking at my door. I grabbed a towel, wiping and drying my tears away. Who could this be, at this time of night? Probably housekeeping, bringing some clean towels or something.

When I opened the door, it was Kenneth standing in my doorway. He grabbed me and hugged me tight, saying, "It's going to be all right. I'm here now, and I've heard everything." All I could do was cry in his arms. Everything was going so wrong. Then, there was Kenneth, the love of my life, there to comfort me.

"Why did you leave me? My life as been so miserable without you," I said, crying.

"I told you to come with me. But you refused to help Nicole out. I'm not going to be in town for long. I know that you're married, but I'm asking you to come with me once again. This time, I'm not leaving without you. I see that your heart's broken and I want to be the one to heal it, with my love. I'm begging you to come with me."

"Kenneth, I'm married. I made a vow, which said 'for better or worse'. I have to make it work out."

"Don't push me away, Regina. Let's start where we left off."

I loved my husband, but I loved Kenneth a little more. He treated me like a lady and gave me a reason to be happy. Kenneth and I lay in the bed together, talking. I missed his wet lips touching my soft skin, his big manly hands rubbing my back and massaging my neck. I could go on.

The next morning when we awakened, the phone started ringing. It was Nicole, saying that Jerome had just called her, looking for me. "He said that he saw your car at a hotel, and he knows Kenneth is in town. He thinks you're with him, so he's on his way there. Regina! Can you hear me?"

"Yeah, I am with Kenneth."

"You might want to warn him because Jerome is highly upset."

When I hung up the phone, I told Kenneth. He looked at me and said, "You're worth fighting for, and more."

"I don't want you two fighting over me. Besides, me and you don't have anything going on, but Jerome wouldn't see it that way."

Kenneth grabbed my hand and kissed it, saying, "You don't have anything to worry about, because what I have to say may shock you or upset you. Do you think you will be able to handle it?"

"It depends on what you have to say."

Just as Kenneth was about to say something, there was a knock on the door. Suddenly, they said, "Regina, I know you're in there with Kenneth." The knocking began to turn into loud bangs. I tried talking to Jerome from inside, but he insisted that I let him in or he was going to knock the door down. So, I opened the door.

Jerome and Kenneth eyeballed each other, up and down. "What's going on?" Jerome said. "Nothing, me and Kenneth were getting ready to go down for breakfast." I grabbed my purse, and Kenneth's hand and headed out the door.

"You're still my wife, and that makes you a married woman!"

I stopped and took off my wedding band and threw it at Jerome.

After me and Kenneth ate breakfast, I took him to my salon.

"So, all this time," I said, "you have been single."

"No," Kenneth said. "I'm not going to lie to you. I have had relationships, on and off. But I never let them get serious because I always wanted to be with you. Out of all the women that I dated, none of them compared to you."

That's what I loved about Kenneth. He was always honest with me, no matter what. He would always tell me the truth, whether it was good or bad. Since Shebba was Kenneth's cousin, I thought he might know a little about her, so I asked him if he knew anything about her messing around with Jerome. Kenneth didn't want to see me hurting no more than I already was, but that was a part of life that everyone has to go through. Like Nicole said, everyone gets a chance to be loved and hurt.

Kenneth and me went to his mom's house. While Kenneth and me were in the kitchen, Shebba walks in.

"Regina, did you know that you have two flat tires?"

"No," I said. "That's just how my tires look."

"As flat as a pancake," Shebba said.

I went outside to look. 'Whore' was written on my front window. The first person's name that popped in my head was Shebba's. Kenneth said that it could have been anybody.

"Don't take up for her. I know that it was her, and I also know that blood is thicker than water."

Kenneth fixed my tires and said that he would deal with her later.

We went back to my hotel and talked and talked, that turned into us between the sheets, making sweet love. Later on that night the phone rang. It was Jerome, telling me in a sad voice that his mother had just died in a car wreck.

"This better not be a joke, Jerome."

"It's not. Turn on the news."

I jumped out of bed, putting my clothes on.

"Where are you going?" Kenneth said.

"I'm going to the hospital. My husband needs me."

"I need you."

"Now is not the time to be selfish. His mother just died."

While buttoning my shirt, I looked at Kenneth, saying, "I'm sorry about all of this. It just happened."

"What, exactly, are you sorry about? Jerome's mother dying or sleeping with me?"

I looked at him and said, "Both."

"You wanted this to happen, just as much as I did."

"No, Kenneth, I didn't. You know that I'm going through some things in my marriage, and I think the only reason I slept with you was to make Jerome mad."

"So, you used me for revenge?" Kenneth asked, angrily.

"Not exactly. I love you, but I belong to him."

"You're confused, Regina. You're so confused that you're saying anything."

I tried giving Kenneth a kiss, but he just turned his head. I was hurting, and I was hurting the people I loved and that loved me. Deep down inside, I cared about Kenneth and I loved him more than words could say. Why I left him lying in the bed of the hotel that night to go comfort my husband that hurt me over and over again, I don't know. And I guess I will never know.

Chapter Seven

Don't think that I went back to Jerome.

I moved back in with my mother. She was still hurting from losing her best friend. The only person I was willing to be there for was my mother. From time to time, Jerome and me would go out. I guess I thought that may help restore our marriage, by us being separated, although it did seem like Jerome was growing up. But I still couldn't fully put my trust in him.

My best friend suggested that I go for Kenneth. She said some people don't get a second chance at love, and especially with the same person. She also stated that Kenneth would be leaving in two days. She handed me a letter from Kenneth. I laid the letter on the table, not bothering to open it.

Nicole announced that she was tying the knot this weekend. I congratulated her with a hug. She asked for me to be her bridesmaid, which I gladly accepted. I was so happy for Nicole. Actually, I think that I was happier for her than I was for myself when I got married. The next day, I went to work at my salon and Jerome's ex-girlfriend walked in. While I was fixing her hair, she started talking about Jerome. She asked if we were still together. She assumed that I was the reason they split up. But I made it clear to her that it was already over before I came along.

"So, you just thought that you could come along and make it worse. I was crazy about Jerome until I found out that he was messing around on me with you and all the other women."

"What are you talking about? You can't possibly love Jerome the way that I do," I said, angrily.

"Regina, me and Jerome share a history together. My love for him is way stronger than what you have for him. Like I said before, we have a history together. I seemed to think things were getting better between us until he told me that he was leaving me for another woman, which happened to of been you. There were times that he would make up an argument over nothing. He started sleeping on the couch, and would pause when I told him that I loved him. But I'm glad you took that good-for-nothing man off my shoulders. You grabbed yourself a headache every night. So, how's things?" she said.

"Things are great between me and Jerome. Did you know that we were married?"

Jerome's ex jumped up out of the seat saying, "That wedding band on your finger don't mean shit! I mean, for other people it might mean something, but for you it's nothing. Jerome will come back to me, you'll see."

I had a feeling Jerome's ex was trying to tell me something. Why couldn't she just spit it out? I couldn't believe that he had treated her the same way that he'd treated me.

"By the way, I didn't quite catch your name."

"It's Katrina."

As she was handing me some money, I noticed a wedding ring on her finger. "You're married," I said.

"Yeah."

"Then why are you so worried about who Jerome is with?"

"You asked too many questions, but you'll soon find the answer to them," Katrina said, walking off.

I thought she was crazy. But pretty. She had long black hair that hung down her back. Green eyes that would hypnotize most guys, slim waist, and thick in all the right places. I thought if I bought myself some long weave, green contacts, and a girdle that I could look like her. But I stopped myself right there. Even if I was to look as beautiful as her, Jerome would still treat me the same way. I realized looks had nothing to do with it, because even pretty girls get treated bad by guys. It had nothing to do with me being poor or rich, fat or skinny, or dumb or smart. Jerome was a dog. And someone had to teach him a lesson.

Suddenly, the phone started ringing. It was Nicole saying, "Rumor is, you and Jerome are getting back together. Is it true, Regina?"

"Well, we talked about it."

"Open up your eyes, Regina. Just open them up wide and take a good look around you. Anyone that keeps you crying throughout the night does not love you. He may say he does, but actions speak louder than words. What I'm trying to say is, a one-night stand man can tell you he loves you but do you honestly think he means it? Kenneth is leaving real soon, and I hope you wake up before it's too late."

"Nicole, I am grown, and whoever I chose to be with is my business. It's my life," I said.

"But don't you want better out of life? You deserve better. We make mistakes to learn from them, not to repeat them over and over again. But you know what? It is your life, and I'm not going to sit around and watch you get made a fool out of. My wedding is soon; I just hope you'll be there. Like they say, love is blind, and you're living proof. Remember, when I was in your shoes? I gave this one guy money every time he would ask for it, and the only thing he gave me was an empty savings account."

"OK, Nicole. I hear you."

"I hope that you listen."

After getting off the phone with Nicole, I went into the bathroom, remembering wishing on a falling star, which was for Kenneth to come back to me. And, it came true. Now, I act as if I don't even want him. A lot of people make wishes all the time, but only some of the wishes come true. I should be grateful. I wanted to run to Kenneth and tell him that I was sorry, and how I felt about him. All of a sudden, I remembered Nicole giving me a letter from Kenneth. So, I left my shop and drove home.

As I began opening the letter, I could smell Kenneth's cologne on it. All I could think that it said was that he didn't want to see me again. It read *I still love you, Regina, although you hurt me that night that you left me alone in a hotel. What I have been trying to tell you might upset you, but I feel that you have a right to know. I mean, everyone else knows. Jerome is cheating on you with Shebba. Don't think that I would tell you this to break you two up, or hurt you so you would be with me. Everything happens for a reason, and I think this happened so that we could be together again.*

I was so mad that I ripped up the letter into pieces. After, a while from being terribly upset, I called Jerome, asking him if he needed a ride. Like I said before, someone needed to teach him a lesson, and that person was me. Before I drove to pick him up, I grabbed my gun and put it underneath the driver's seat. While I was driving Jerome from work, I looked at him and said, "I know everything, Jerome."

Jerome pretended not to know what I was talking about, until I said, "I know that you're cheating on me with Shebba. Yeah, I heard all about your dirt that you swept to the side."

"Well, I haven't been completely honest in our marriage. I have a confession to make, but don't get mad. I have been cheating on you with Shebba."

"The town's whore!" I yelled. How could he tell me not to get mad? How was I supposed to react?

"How could you, Jerome? I gave you my heart and you stepped all over it," I said, crying. "Was I not enough woman for you, that you had to be with other women? Did you want me to gain some weight? What was it?"

"It wasn't you, Regina. It was me. Shebba threw herself at me, and she was very tempting. I just fell for temptation."

"Jerome, are you stupid? What appears pretty on the outside isn't always good for you."

"She came after me first. I turned her down a lot of times."

"You, being the dog that you are, just had to give in. How long has it been going on?" I asked.

"For three months. But it's over. I have changed for you."

How was I supposed to believe that, when all he had been feeding me was lies? I was so mad that I couldn't even think straight. I pushed my foot on the gas pedal and started going fast.

"Don't kill us!" Jerome yelled out.

"Why not? Our vow said 'til death do us part. Why not die together? Why, Jerome?"

"I don't know," he said.

"Maybe this will help you remember the question better."

I grabbed my gun from underneath my seat and said once again, "Why, Jerome?"

"Because, like you said, I'm stupid! I wasn't thinking."

"Can you give me back my heart that you stole from me?"

"I would if I could. I would even give you mine."

"Jerome, you don't even have a heart! Open the door."

"What?"

"Open the door and jump out." It's funny how one man can change you and make you have so much anger hatred inside your heart. Men can make you do so many crazy things. Just as I was about to pull the trigger, Jerome jumped out.

We were over a big body of water. I started slowing down. I wasn't really going to shoot him; I didn't even have any bullets. I wasn't going to prison over murder; I'm smarter than that. I just wanted to scare him and make him realize that you can't just go around playing with people's minds, bodies, and souls. Some of us can't take it, and some of us can. His ex-committed suicide. Like they say, what comes around goes around, twice as bad.

Jerome was saved by some fishermen. He told everyone that he jumped out of the car on his own because he was trying to commit suicide, but of course I know the real story. I think that I know Jerome will be a better man, but not for me. I just hope that I made him a better man for someone else.

Chapter Eight

I was still hurting from Jerome. I told Nicole that I wasn't going to be able to attend her wedding, because I was going away with Kenneth.

"Well, that's a good excuse not to attend," she said.

I wished her the best and hoped she wouldn't be treated the way I have. But I wasn't leaving yet. I had someone else to take care of.

I went to my beauty salon and put up the 'Open' sign. Everyone that came by, I turned them away. I was doing a special style for someone, and nothing or no one was going to stand in my way. I sat in my chair and waited and waited. I guess she wasn't coming. Nicole called my cell saying that Kenneth was looking for me.

"Where are you, Regina? Kenneth's at the bus stop. Don't tell me that you changed your mind."

"No, I'm on my way to the bus stop. I just forgot something."

"Well hurry, all right?"

"Bye."

I didn't want to tell Nicole what was up my sleeve. She would just try to convince me otherwise. After I hung up the phone, I grabbed my purse. I put up the 'Closed' sign, and started walking out the door. Then, there she was. Shebba.

"Are you closing?" she asked.

"Oh no! Not since you're here! Things were just a little slow."

"So, have you and Jerome solved your problems?"

"Sort of," I said. I have only one more problem to solve."

I started putting Shebba's perm in her hair, and asking her questions.

"Do you know what it feels to be in love with someone for a long period of time, and then just have them cheat on you with someone they barely even know?"

"I have never been in that situation," Shebba said, smacking on her gum. After I was done with her, she was going to be choking on it.

My final question to her was, "Have you ever slept with Jerome?"

"No!" she said, smiling. If only she could have been a woman and told the truth. Like they say, the truth shall set you free. She just grinned about it, not caring or realizing how hurt I was inside. I grabbed my keys and started walking off.

"Where are you going?" Shebba said, standing up.

"I'm going to get something to drink."

"But you have a drink machine right here."

"It's out of drinks. I'll be back."

I shut the door and locked it behind me. Rule #1: Don't ever get your hair done by the woman whose man you're sleeping with. That was a mistake. I took my toolbox around back and turned off the water. You can just imagine what was about to happen. You may call it cruel, but I call it revenge. Maybe that will teach her a lesson, not to ever mess with another woman's man, because you never know what you're getting yourself into, or the consequences you will have to pay. What may appear harmless, sweet, and innocent can be the total opposite.

I waited for a half hour before I turned the water back on. I went back inside. Shebba was crying, pouring into her hair bottles of water that she had bought from the machine. "Did you know that they turned your water off?"

"No, and I didn't know that my husband was cheating on me with you!"

"I'm sorry Regina. Just get this out of my head!"

"Shebba, can you feel the pain that I'm feeling?"

"I'm sorry, I never meant to hurt you."

I grabbed Shebba. "You meant to hurt me or you wouldn't have done it. You knew he wasn't yours. This is for all the women whose men you have messed around with. You hurt them as well. It's over between us. I really don't care now."

While washing Shebba's hair, I could see her hair was falling out.

"What have you done to my hair?" she said, with strands of hair in her hand.

"I just gave you a new style. You know bald is 'in'. If you're not happy with that, I have lots of wigs for you to choose from." Shebba straightened the wig on her head. "You are one crazy bitch," she said, walking out the door.

I was having so much fun that I almost forgot about Kenneth. I grabbed my bags and called a taxi. When I arrived, they said, "Kenneth's bus just took off." I ran after the bus, hoping someone would see me and convince the driver to stop, but the bus just started going faster and faster, leaving me tired and far behind. I stopped running and started huffing and puffing, looking back at the last bus in sight. I turned around with my bags in my hand, thinking to myself *I should just get on the bus and go wherever it takes me.*

And that's just what I did. I sat on the bus, wondering where my new life was going to start. Somewhere where I knew no one or had no one. Kenneth had vanished out of my life once again. I never got to tell him how much I loved him, and cared. I couldn't erase Kenneth off my mind. No matter how hard I would try, he would always remain somewhere in my heart.

I grabbed my pillow and Walkman out of my bag. Resting my head on my pillow and listening to Kenneth's and my favorite song, my eyes became watery. After the song went off, I went to the bathroom. Just as I was opening the bathroom door, I could hear someone calling my name.

Was there someone else named Regina on the bus? I looked back and it was Kenneth, the love of my life.

I ran to him and we held each other tight. Everyone stared at us, as if it was a fight. I looked at them, smiling, saying, "Everything is all right." We sat on the bus, as the driver continued driving. My cell phone rang numerous times. "Who could this be?" I said, holding my phone. It was Nicole. I didn't bother answering it.

When we arrived at Kenneth's place, he said, "Have you ever loved someone so much that you would do anything, just to have them in your life?" I smiled, saying, 'I would have done anything to have you back in my life, but I only would have taken it to a certain limit. Why, Kenneth?"

"There are no limits that you want to cross, when you're in love," Kenneth said.

Days went by and I had been with Kenneth for two weeks, and no one had called me. I looked around for my cell phone, but it was nowhere in sight.

"Kenneth, have you seen my cell?"

"No, baby," Kenneth said, leaving for class.

I hadn't heard from my mother or Nicole in a while, so I gave them a call. Nicole said, "I have been trying to call you."

"What's wrong?"

"Shebba told everything."

"She deserved it."

"No, I'm talking about Kenneth."

"What about Kenneth?"

"Just go look for something important in his house."

"What am I supposed to be looking for? Nicole, you are starting to scare me. What's wrong?"

"You are not married to Jerome. You never have been. His ex, Katrina, is officially married to him."

"What? I have a wedding band on. I'm married. I got married at a small church, by a priest."

"He wasn't a real priest."

"If this is all true, why would Jerome pretend to be married to me?"

"I don't know, but Kenneth is behind all of this, somewhere. He paid Shebba to sleep with Jerome to ruin your marriage. She told me."

"Why would he do that?"

"He didn't want you with anybody but him. He's obsessed with you."

"That's crazy."

She said something about everything was in a black box. "OK, 'bye."

I ran back home. I opened the drawers, throwing Kenneth's clothes everywhere. I looked under the bed. I looked almost everywhere. Then, there it was. A black shoe box. I opened it and found pictures of Jerome and me. He had taken my cell phone and turned it off. I found letters that Shebba and Kenneth had written to one another, tapes from the answering machine. And major cash.

Suddenly, Kenneth's phone started ringing. I ran to answer it. It was Kenneth, asking me if I had found my cell phone.

"No, maybe someone stole it. You know what?" I said. "I have a big surprise for you."

He said, "What is it?"

"Come home and see, you can't miss seeing it."

I went back to Kenneth's room, playing the tapes. Jerome was saying for Kenneth to pay Jerome $20,000 to pretend to marry me. Another tape was them arguing about Kenneth only giving Jerome $10,000, so the plan was off. *Why would Kenneth do this?* I said to myself. That's what I was trying to find out. I was so upset, I didn't know what to do. I laid all of the letters and stuff in the middle of the floor and lit a match. I sat there and watched them burn. Then the fire began to spread. I didn't care, because I was mad as hell. The man I thought loved me set me up for happiness and heartbreak. Do you really call that love?

I left and watched Kenneth pull in the driveway. I called him on his cell and said, "Surprise! I told you that you couldn't miss it!" I hung up and went back home.

My mom said, "The things some women will do when they're fed up. Some of us slash tires, break or spray paint car windows, play on the phone, and just act a damn fool. But the sweet, quiet, innocent ones let all that anger build up inside of them and burn a house down. So, Regina. What did you learn out of all of this?"

"Not to ever trust a man," I said.

"All men are not the same, honey. They are all different. Some of them pretend to be players in front of their friends and some of them just need a good woman in their life to help guide them in the right direction. There're some men out there that have been down your road—cheated on, heartbroken, left alone with kids—because their baby's momma was a junkie, or a drunk, whore, or anything. There are some men out there, looking for a good woman just like you. Someone that they can hold at night, someone to cook for them, and a good mother to help take care of their kids. A person can change a person by the way that they're treated. Just like drugs change people."

"My point is that I don't think I'm quite the same person that I was before."

"You changed for the better. Now you don't take no mess."

My mom said that I would find a man with no games. "That's the one you want, because at least you know he can't play you if he has no games." I laughed.

But I found happiness and his name is Dill Doe. Well, for a while. A woman can't live without a man as well as a man can't live without a woman.

A couple months later, I decided to change my life around by going to church every Sunday, and getting down on my knees and praying to God. Those were the things that I didn't do when my marriage was in trouble.

Three months ago, I was blessed with a good man, a bigger salon, and a beautiful baby boy. It's amazing how good things can happen to you when you put God first. For everyone who has a good woman or man: love him or her each and every day and let him or her know you appreciate everything.